# Have You Ever Thou~
## Teachers Who Are Extra-weird
## Might Also Be Extr~

*Quiz Yourself:*

1. You've forgotten your homework. Your teacher says:
   a. "Stay after school."
   b. "I want a note from your mother."
   c. "Maybe it's time to upgrade that memory chip I planted in your brain!"

2. The broken loudspeaker in your classroom is making deafening screeches. Your teacher
   a. dismantles the equipment and tries to fix it.
   b. promptly reports the problem to the janitor.
   c. looks at it and screams, "I've TOLD you not to call me at work!"

If answer "c" sounds familiar, don't panic—just sit down quietly and READ THIS BOOK!

BOOKS IN THE
MY TEACHER IS AN ALIEN SERIES
BY BRUCE COVILLE

My Teacher Is an Alien

My Teacher Fried My Brains

My Teacher Glows in the Dark

My Teacher Flunked the Planet

**ACTION ADVENTURE CD-ROM GAME**
Bruce Coville's My Teacher Is an Alien
*In stores November 1997!*

# Bruce Coville's
# IS YOUR TEACHER
# AN ALIEN?

with **Lisa Meltzer**
and
**Larissa Harris**

Illustrated by John Pierard

BYRON PREISS MULTIMEDIA COMPANY, INC.
NEW YORK

POCKET BOOKS
NEW YORK    LONDON    TORONTO    SYDNEY    TOKYO    SINGAPORE

An *Original* Publication of POCKET BOOKS

 POCKET BOOKS, a division of Simon and Schuster Inc., 1230 Avenue of the Americas, New York, NY 10020

Copyright ©1997 by Byron Preiss Multimedia Company, Inc.
Published by arrangement with General Licensing Company, Inc.

Byron Preiss Multimedia Company, Inc.
24 West 25th Streeet
New York, NY 10010

Mazes used with permission of Sterling Publishing Co., Inc., 387 Park Ave. S., NY, NY 10016 from *Mystifying Math Puzzles* by Steve Ryan, © 1996 by Steve Ryan and *Pencil Puzzlers* by Steve Ryan, © 1992 by Steve Ryan.

The Byron Preiss Multimedia World Wide Web Site address is:
**http://www.byronpreiss.com**

The Is Your Teacher an Alien? Web Site address is
**http://www.byronpreiss.com/alien**

ISBN 0-671-01184-7
First Pocket Books paperback printing December 1997
10 9 8 7 6 5 4 3 2 1
POCKET and colophon are registered trademarks of Simon and Schuster Inc.

Cover art by Steve Fastner
Cover design by Steven Jablonoski
Interior design by MM Design 2000, Inc.
Developed by Byron Preiss and Daniel Weiss

Printed in the U.S.A.

# Greetings, Fellow Students . . .

Many of you may remember us from the My Teacher Is an Alien series. It all started when our sixth-grade teacher, Ms. Schwartz, disappeared. Susan Simmons discovered that "Mr. Smith," our substitute teacher, was really an alien named Broxholm, who was planning to kidnap five kids from our class and take them into space to study them. Of course, she could barely believe it! She knew it would be practically impossible to convince the rest of the class. First she told Peter Thompson because he was a science fiction fan. But even he needed first-hand evidence. Later we had to let Duncan Dougal, the class bully, in on the amazing secret.

Peter, Duncan, and I formed a pretty unlikely threesome, but, sleuthing together, we tracked our real teacher to Mr. Smith's attic, where she was trapped in a force field! Finally, accidentally—and we won't spoil any more of the story for you—Susan found a way to unmask our alien teacher and chase him out into space.

A lot happened after that. Duncan's brain got fried and he became the class brain (for a change!). We even made friends with some other aliens who wanted to help us and our planet. Finally it was up to the three of us to prove to the Interplanetary Council that Earth and the beings that inhabit it—human beings—should not be blown to bits. We had to convince them that it was worth it to let us live. We succeeded, too—well, we're all still here, aren't we?—but that's a whole other story.

So why are we writing you this note?

Unfortunately some of the aliens aren't cooperating. They've decided to disobey the Council. These rebels believe that we earthlings are just too destructive for our own good, that we're a danger to the rest of the universe. So guess what they're doing?

Yep. You guessed it. At the same time that the Council is sending good aliens to act as teachers, some of the renegades are also posing as teachers, just as Broxholm did. They're showing up in schools around the world and will be trying to abduct kids just like us—that is, kids just like you.

So. If you haven't played it already, try your hand at identifying and escaping from alien teachers with the *My Teacher Is an Alien* CD-ROM game. And check out this handbook. What you'll read will help you recognize whether your teacher is an alien or an ally—and what you can do about it.

The book is divided into a "week," with five sections: Monday, Tuesday, Wednesday, Thursday, and Friday. (No half-days, snow days, or sick days here!)

Each day will be filled with gut-busting goofiness and mind-bending puzzles. Completing the puzzles will bring you clues about whether your teacher is an alien, whether your classmates are androids, how to protect yourself from being kidnapped, and other important information. Good luck on your journey. Think fast. Have fun. And remember, Earth's future is in your hands.

VERY IMPORTANT NOTICE: If your teacher turns out to be an alien, please submit his or her name to our website (www. byronpreiss.com/alien). You see, we'll be tracking down aliens wherever they are and reporting them to the Interplanetary Council.

In friendship,

Susan Simmons,
Peter Thompson,
Duncan Dougal

# MONDAY

# Preliminary Quiz To Determine If Your Teacher Is an Alien

*Think carefully about each question before you answer. Circle only one of the choices.*

1. Trying to be funny, you scrape your fingernails against the blackboard. Your teacher yells:
   a. "Stop that at once!"
   b. "We'll see how the principal likes your little trick!"
   c. "Everybody sing along!"

2. You've forgotten your homework. Your teacher says:
   a. "You must stay after school."
   b. "Maybe it's time to upgrade that memory chip I planted in your brain."
   c. "I want a note from your mother."

3. The new gym teacher's favorite game is:
   a. Red Rover.
   b. Spud.
   c. Destroy the Blue Planet's Major Cities and Exploit Its Natural Resources.

4. Your teacher is planning a field trip. Why are you worried?

a. It may interfere with valuable study time.
b. You have band practice that day.
c. The permission slip says "The school cannot be held responsible for lateness due to traffic, weather conditions, or being sucked into a black hole."

5. During a trip to the planetarium, your teacher is most likely to
a. shush the class.
b. advise you to take notes.
c. jump up and yell, "Lies! It's all a pack of filthy lies!"

6. The broken loudspeaker in your classroom is making deafening screeches. Your teacher
a. dismantles the equipment and tries to fix it.
b. promptly reports the problem to the janitor.
c. looks at it and screams, "I've TOLD you not to call me at work!"

7. Your teacher looks funny today. What is your reaction?
a. You laugh because his tie is crooked.
b. You write a note to your friend about the coffee stain on his shirt.
c. You feel like vomiting all over your desk at the sight of his pea-green complexion.

8. The substitute addresses the class as:
   a. "Class."
   b. "Squishy, two-eyed, fluffy-headed freaks."
   c. "You guys."

9. There's a fight during recess. Your teacher
   a. breaks it up by yelling at the fighters.
   b. breaks it up by grabbing the fighters by their shirts.
   c. breaks it up with a gamma-ray blast from his nostrils.

10. Someone burps in class. Your teacher says:
    a. "Please excuse yourself."
    b. "That is unacceptable classroom behavior."
    c. "Good point, but please speak in complete sentences."

ANSWERS ON PAGE 109

# Preliminary Visual Test to Determine If Your Teacher Is an Alien

*Look closely and circle the one who is different.*

*Note: If you can't find him, we'll wash our hands of you. See you in the spaceship, Spaceball.*

ANSWER ON PAGE 109

# Mind Scramble

You get to school early. In your classroom you see this written on the board:

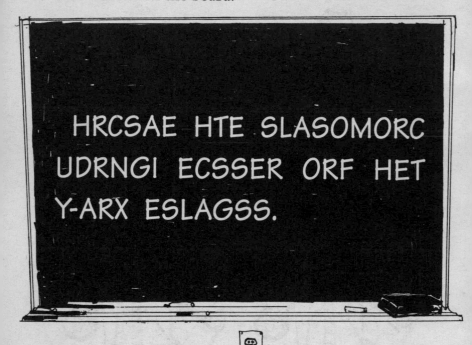

HRCSAE HTE SLASOMORC
UDRNGI ECSSER ORF HET
Y-ARX ESLAGSS.

You write the message down so you can unscramble it on your own. Then you erase it from the board.

*Unscramble the letters and find out what the message says. Hint: Go one word at a time.*

ANSWER ON PAGE 109

# Nutty Note

Next period your friend tries to pass you a note. But—*whoops*—she drops it on the floor. The next thing you know it's in your teacher's hands. Looming over you both, Mrs. Zasloff looks at the note.

She's silent.

You stare at Jen and wonder why she doesn't seem worried.

Mrs. Zasloff turns it upside-down and sideways.

Then she groans and tosses it into the trash can!

As soon as class is over you pick it out of the trash. Now you know why Jen wasn't worried about it being intercepted! You yourself are having a hard time reading it!

*Can you break the code? Hint: look closely at one of the corners for starters.*

ANSWERS ON PAGE 109

# What Is This Thing Called Love?

## A MINI MYSTERY

In social studies class you notice an unfamiliar young woman with long blond hair. She's sitting in the back of the room in front of the map of the American Revolution. Everybody turns to stare at her until Mr. Suransky, your teacher, comes in. You all love Mr. Suransky. He is always making you and your classmates act out the Boston Tea Party or the battle of the Alamo.

"Maybe she's his girlfriend," says Alex, the kid who sits next to you.

"Be quiet, Alex," says Susan Simmons, who sits on the other side of you. "Mr. Suransky has a girl-friend with short dark hair. I saw them at the mall once. This one is more like her opposite. Don't you think?"

She turns to you for agreement.

"I think so," you say, flattered that Susan wants your opinion.

"Definitely," says Susan. "She's probably observing the class for a project, or something."

You like having Susan next to you. She's really smart and always makes the class discussions interesting. Of course, Mr. Suransky likes her. Teachers always like the ones who get involved.

They can't help it.

"Okay, folks," begins Mr. Suransky. "Before we begin, I'd like to introduce you to someone." He gestures toward the woman at the back of the room.

"This is Ms. Love, who will be observing the class today," he says.

Everyone murmurs, "Hi." Ms. Love gives a little wave.

"Ms. Love—uh—I'm sorry, are you from State University, or . . .?" Mr. Suransky says.

"Yes," says the woman. She looks calm and cool. "Yes, I'm from State."

"Would you like to say some words about what you expect to learn?" asks Mr. Suransky. You get the feeling that this was sort of a sudden arrangement. Maybe, just like you, he has no clue who she is.

"Well," says Ms. Love, "I'm interested in children and how they behave."

"Uh-huh," says Mr. Suransky. He frowns slightly. "Are you writing a paper, or . . .?"

"I'm really just here to observe," says Ms. Love, smiling sweetly.

"Well! You'll certainly find a wide variety of behaviors here!" says Mr. Suransky.

Everyone laughs, except, you notice, Ms. Love herself. She just continues to smile.

The whole class has been looking back and forth, from Mr. Suransky to Ms. Love, as if they are watching a tennis match. Now that their conversation seems to be over, Susan leans over to you and says, "She's being kind of vague, don't you think?"

You agree.

"I mean," she continues, with one eye on the young woman, "is she really dumb or is she really scary—that's my question."

"How would we be able to tell?" you ask. You know what she's talking about. "Really scary" has a special meaning around here these days.

"No talking please," says Mr. Suransky. This is directed at you and Susan. "Today we'll continue to talk about the colonies' fight for independence. Just to make sure everybody's with me . . ." He looks around the room. "Marian, can you tell us who the redcoats were?"

So class goes on in a pretty normal way. But Mr. Suransky seems a bit intimidated by the strange young woman in the back of the room. What's up with her? you wonder.

When class is over, Mr. Suransky tilts his head and clears his throat. You've come to recognize this gesture as an announcement that he's about to make a joke.

"Extra credit," he announces. Everybody falls silent.

"Here's a complicated research question for you," he says. "Can anybody tell me if there's a fourth of July in France?"

Everybody, except for Ms. Love, is immediately animated. Mr. Suransky allows a minute of discussion and then asks what everybody's come up with. There's a flurry of yeses and noes and a lot of giggling because everyone suspects it's a joke. But no one is sure. Mr. Suransky silences you all with a raised hand. "In order to solve this dispute, shall we ask our guest to answer the question?"

He smiles reassuringly at Ms. Love.

"Well," she says, "There is a holiday for French independence, but no, as far as I know there is no Fourth of July in France."

The look on Mr. Suransky's face is hard to read. "Folks, give me your answers tomorrow, and we'll figure everything out then," he says. He turns around and starts erasing the board furiously.

Susan turns to you. "I'm still not absolutely sure," she says, "but I'm leaning toward really scary."

*Why has Susan come to this conclusion?*

ANSWER ON PAGE 109

# Noodle Fool-you-dle

You usually don't pay much attention to the food they serve at school but today you notice the noodles doing strange things on the plate.

*Which way are those noodles facing?*

**ANSWER ON PAGE 109**

# Sneak Peek

Finally it's recess. You ask to go to the bathroom. Now's your chance to search your empty classroom for the X-ray glasses.

*Search well—make contact with every star.*

ANSWER ON PAGE 110

Hey!
Turn
Around!

# Pix Tricks #1

Just before Mrs. Howard's class you remember Jen's note. It said to meet her at her locker before class started. Jen's not at her locker, but taped to the outside is this note.

*Can you figure out what it says?*

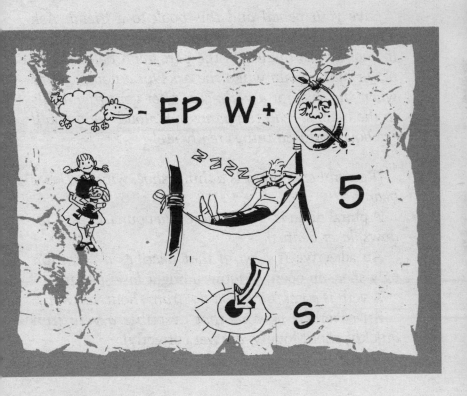

ANSWER ON PAGE 110

# Speed Read

You're having a hard time concentrating in Mrs. Howard's class (big surprise). You read your book report aloud to the class and, unfortunately, it comes out sounding strange.

*Give your pencil and this book to a friend. Ask your friend to tell you the type of word needed to fill in each of the blanks in the paragraph below. Give her or him a noun when she asks for a noun, a verb when she asks for a verb, etc. After your friend fills in the blanks, read the paragraph aloud—and you'll see how confused things really are!*

*(Remember: a* noun *is a thing (shoe, window, laser beam).*

*A* plural noun *is two or more of a noun (shoes, windows, laser beams).*

*An* adjective *is a word that decribes a noun (an ugly shoe, an open window, a bright laser beam).*

*A* verb *is something you do (run, shout, answer).*

*An* adverb *is a word that describes a verb (run quickly, shout loudly, answer correctly).*

The book I read was called The _three_ _animals_.
                                     adjective   noun

The main characters were a _pig_, a _wolf_, and
                            noun      noun

a _tiger_. They go to _woods_ and _run_ until
    noun              place        verb

their _energy_ runs out. They meet _3_
         noun                        number

_lions_ and are very scared. They try very hard
plural noun

to _____ and _____. One of the characters is not
    verb       verb

able to stop _____ ing. Soon they discover a secret
              verb

_____ _____ and can _____ escape. They
adjective  noun        adverb

_____ home and are welcomed _____, with
verb                          adverb

great joy and _____. The _____ of the story is:
               noun        noun

Never _____ your _____.
        verb        noun

17

# Cheat Sheet!

Phew! The last period of the day is finally over and you're out of there! As the bell rings and everyone hurries out of school, a piece of paper falls out of a teacher's bag. You pick it up and smooth it out. You see it's a cheat sheet, written in a strange, clear handwriting that just couldn't be a kid's.

*These are phrases and facts that YOU should know. YOU are the one from Earth, after all. If you can figure out what the initials stand for, congratulations—you've broken the code.*

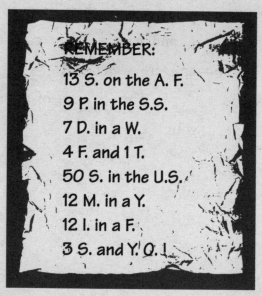

REMEMBER:

13 S. on the A. F.

9 P. in the S.S.

7 D. in a W.

4 F. and 1 T.

50 S. in the U.S.

12 M. in a Y.

12 I. in a F.

3 S. and Y. O. !

ANSWERS ON PAGE 110

# A Lot Out of a Little

You look around at the kids in the hall. They all look as normal as ever—some more than others. Are you making something out of nothing?

*See how many words you can make out of the word "nothingness."*

# N O T H I N G N E S S

ANSWERS ON PAGE 110

# Scareway

You're running down the steps to get to the school-bus. Suddenly you realize you've been running longer than you should. You stop and look at the steps very carefully. Up and down. Then you look at them even more carefully. Yipes! Which is the top step and which is the bottom step?

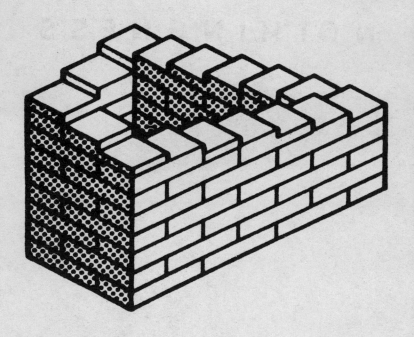

ANSWER ON PAGE 111

On the bus going home you tell Duncan Dougal you're really getting nervous, knowing he's dealt with aliens before—and all he does is grunt and recite this list. How obnoxious!

## Duncan's Top Ten Reasons Why He Wouldn't Mind Being Abducted After All

1. Alien flesh feels really cool when you punch it.
2. Susan Simmons has seen me cry!
3. I could come back and trap Ms. Schwartz in a forcefield, just for old times' sake.
4. I wouldn't have to wait until my sixteenth birthday to drive my own saucer.
5. The aliens and I have similar taste in music. Bad, that is.
6. I could "space out" whenever I wanted. Ha, ha.
7. Peter will be there to pick on for eternity, in case the aliens are too strong.
8. I've always wanted to sneeze in zero gravity!
9. I could finally be known as "Darth" instead of "Dougal"!
10. Since I'll never be home, I'll never have home-work.

# TUESDAY

# Morning Warning

This morning you feel as if you should tell some-body something about the weird situation at school. So before you leave the house, you sit down and write a note for your mom. She'll read it when she gets home from work.

*This time have a friend fill in the blanks with the right type of word, and then read the note back to you. (For more instructions, go back to page 16.)*

Dear Mom,

I am writing this _____ to warn you of a _____
                  noun                          adjective

problem. Yesterday I saw my teacher _____ing
                                        verb

with a _____. I found a _____ next to the
       noun                noun

_____ in my classroom. There were also strange
noun

_____ in the girls' _____. You might not
plural noun            noun

believe me, but I really saw the _____ _____ and
                                noun    verb

I'm afraid if we don't _____ right away there could
                  verb

be some _____ _____ on our hands. Please
      adjective   plural noun

take this seriously, because otherwise major

_____ might _____.
plural noun         verb

Your _____ _____
    adjective   noun

24

# Headlight Headache

You get off the schoolbus this morning and happen to notice the headlights. They don't seem quite right.

*Are the rings in the headlights pointing up, or are they pointing down?*

ANSWER ON PAGE 111

# Teacher Creature

As you walk into school, you pass by the teacher's lounge. The three teachers in there sure look weird. They remind you of a movie . . . but something's a little off.

*Look at the picture and the first initials for your clues. Then see if you can fill in the letter blanks.*

T_____ M_____ N____ T_____

ANSWER ON PAGE 111

# Survival Guide

Though you try not to be paranoid, you can't stop wondering about what you'll need to survive if you're captured by aliens. Here are some things you'll DEFINITELY need—and some things you probably won't.

*Find these hidden words and you'll be safe—at least for a little while.*

```
D L S N I A R B O V E R
O I M Q R P E L G Y F O
G X S U L B A O P R O T
S P Y G I L O W V E H A
M Y R G U V Q D S O S L
O A U T E I O R E G A S
N U P H A N S Y D O I N
E E R D O O F E A R Y A
Y O N W A T E R M O T R
B T U S L I N G S H O T
```

food, water, slingshot, disguise, brains, blowdryer, money, translator, map, oxygen

ANSWERS ON PAGE 111

# For Your Eyes Only

Yesterday you pulled off staying in for recess. Today you say "your stomach hurts"—this is truer than you want it to be—and it works! Now's your chance to use the X-ray glasses you found to search your teacher's desk!

*Can you find these objects?*

pen
five pencils
extra mask
extra "gloves"
set of teeth
pair of eyeballs
ruler
ruler with weird measurements
ray gun
Frisbee
Walkman
computer game
mini eyeball-washing machine
lie detector
cosmetic cream
unidentifiable instrument
three reference books you might find in an alien
    library
small fuzzy animal
pictures of alien family back home

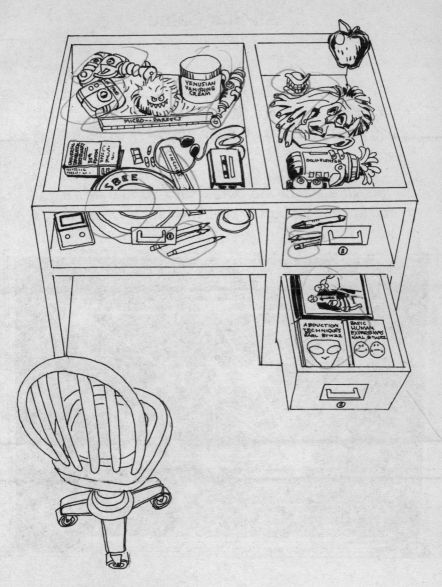

ANSWERS ON PAGE 112

# All-Star Game

Your next period is math. You come in and see this puzzle on the board. It's suspiciously galactic-looking, but it also looks kind of fun.

*Your assignment is to put the numbers one through eight in the blank stars so that when you add up the numbers in each row of three stars, they'll equal fifteen.*

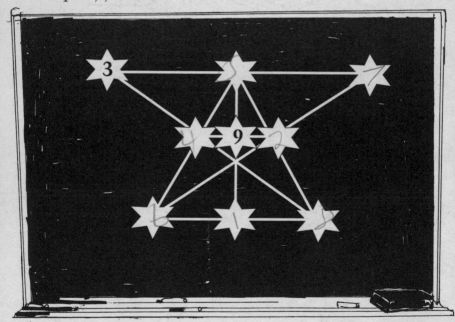

ANSWER ON PAGE 112

# The Case of the Suspicious Substitute

You come into science class and sit down in your seat. Trying to remember what your homework was, you lean down and start searching through your backpack. You feel a tap on your shoulder. You look up.

"Hey," says Peter Thompson. You like sitting next to Peter. He's friendly and doesn't mind slipping you some hints once in a while. "How's it going?" he says, sitting down in his seat.

"Okay," you say, continuing to rummage through the big inside pocket of your backpack.

"I heard we have a sub today," says Peter's voice above you. You sit up with relief.

Peter looks bummed. "We were going to talk about photosynthesis," he says.

By this time the fact that there's going to be a sub has spread around the room and everyone is getting in the mood. No one seems to think a substitute might be a bad sign (as in, a bad sign for life on Earth). The door opens and the sub walks in. Suddenly everybody quiets down to get a good look.

The sub is a tall, red-haired, strong-looking guy, wearing what seems to be a safari outfit—his shirt has about twenty pockets on it. He strides right to the desk, slaps it, and stands there for about a minute. Finally he begins:

31

"Hello, everybody. My name is Mr. Forsythe and I'm going to be your substitute today, as I'm sure most of you realize. Don't get too excited—we'll be following Ms. Wan's lesson plan and studying photosynthesis."

Peter sits up excitedly.

"Mr. Forsythe, what do you do when you're not a sub?" shouts someone in the back of the room.

A very basic stalling tactic, of course. But Mr Forsythe takes the bait.

"Well actually . . . uh . . . ," he says, glancing at the names on the seating chart, "I'm in graduate school, Josh. I study biology."

"Wow," Josh says dubiously.

"'Wow' is right," says the sub. "Now please turn to page forty-six in your textbook."

Then Peter, who usually doesn't participate much in substitute games, raises his hand. "What kinds of things do you study?" he blurts out.

Maybe the sub can tell Peter's truly interested, because he doesn't look annoyed. He tells us he studies ecosystems, which are communities of organisms in their natural environments. "I study many different kinds of organisms," he says, looking around the room. This statement makes you feel a little weird, but Peter is unfazed. He asks Mr. Forsythe which ecosystem he has studied most recently.

"The prairies in Argentina," says the sub. "The people there call them Las Pampas."

"Did you rope cattle and stuff?" somebody else asks.

"Did I rope cattle? I did, as a matter of fact," the sub says, and leans against the desk. "Now back to page forty-six."

But no one pays attention. "Mr. Forsythe, were you a cowboy?" Julie Chamovitz yells, and everybody laughs.

"Well actually . . . uh . . . Julie," he begins, "There are cowboys on Las Pampas, you know, but they're known as gauchos. Let me write it on the board."

"Tell us a story from the Pampas!" yells Jordan from the back. Everybody laughs at her pronunciation of the word "Pampas" which, you have to admit, sounds something like the word "Pampers."

"C'mon," you all say, and Mr. Forsythe relents.

"Once, in December or January," he begins, "some other researchers and I were huddled in a little hut trying to keep warm. It was nighttime and the Argentine winters are bitter cold. Anyway, we heard a strange, low sound outside. It happened again, and then again. We all looked at each other, hoping that someone else would go investigate. But no one budged. Then the sound came again, over the howling of the prairie wind. The hut began to shake. Something was pushing against the walls, trying to get in! We looked at each other in horror. Finally I was chosen to go out into the night and scare whatever it was away."

He pauses for effect.

"I ventured out into the freezing wind and what did I find? Only a cow, who had strayed from her herd and wandered toward our light. We let her inside, and she lay down and went right to sleep."

Everyone is pretty satisfied with that story, but not satisfied enough to turn to page forty-six. You glance at Peter and notice he's frowning. His chin is in his hands and he's staring at the teacher without blinking. What's going on with him? He can't just be disappointed over not hearing about photosynthesis. You wonder if he suspects this teacher of something more serious than being a pushover. But how could he? Mr. Forsythe sure seems like a real live substitute.

After class is over, and people are milling around, you lean over to Peter. "Yo," you say.

"Huh?" says Peter. He's still in a semi-frozen position.

"Peter, what's freaking you out?" you say.

"You know what?" he says with a stricken look. "Mr. Forsythe was lying about Argentina. He's never even been there. I'm very afraid that Ms. Wan isn't coming back and that Mr. Forsythe is the reason."

*How does Peter know that Mr. Forsythe has never been to Argentina?*

ANSWER ON PAGE 113

# Word Warp

If any of these words describe your teacher . . . you're in trouble! *Can you find them all?*

| | | | |
|---|---|---|---|
| braindead | disguised | greasy | greenish |
| gross | hairy | invisible | mutant |
| nutty | prickly | slimy | rude |
| scary | sinister | smelly | spacy |
| spotted | wacky | weird | wobbly |

```
M  N  I  E  S  X  C  I  H  V  M  C  H  T  P  O  Q
S  P  O  D  Y  D  K  E  P  S  C  S  N  Z  W  V  L
H  S  J  S  L  I  M  Y  L  B  M  V  T  O  N  I  K
D  P  Z  C  U  S  Y  S  A  E  R  G  B  C  Y  C  N
P  O  P  A  Z  G  B  D  L  X  F  B  Z  T  Y  L  V
A  T  B  R  E  U  L  L  S  D  L  I  T  B  K  S  O
K  T  S  Y  Y  I  Y  E  K  Y  I  U  Q  Y  A  V  D
X  E  Y  K  G  S  K  G  S  I  N  I  S  T  E  R  H
S  D  C  S  M  E  I  E  S  E  V  N  X  S  R  E  I
U  A  A  H  E  D  H  D  O  R  I  L  D  E  F  T  E
W  G  P  A  L  C  N  U  R  G  S  M  S  R  K  X  S
T  H  S  I  N  E  E  R  G  T  I  N  G  Y  I  H  T
S  N  I  R  X  Z  M  N  M  K  B  F  O  B  R  E  J
Y  E  A  Y  T  C  J  S  V  C  L  J  X  M  B  U  M
G  Q  E  T  K  P  E  M  D  A  E  D  N  I  A  R  B
Z  H  D  F  U  P  R  I  C  K  L  Y  C  D  I  V  M
R  X  S  C  G  M  V  S  P  V  H  K  P  E  C  S  X
```

SOLUTION ON PAGE 113

At this point it seems pretty clear that some of your teachers are not from Earth. Yesterday Duncan Dougal didn't have much to say, but Susan Simmons, who is usually more helpful than Duncan, has come up with these bits of advice.

## Susan's Helpful Hints For Coping With Alien Teachers

1. First, a safety tip: Bring to school the lead pad that your dentist puts on you when he takes X-rays, if you can sneak it out of his office. It provides protection from Alien Teacher Glare Radiation Syndrome (ATGRS).

2. Pretend you're an alien. Tug on your face. Eat lots of dust bunnies and a mothball or two a day—or at least fake it. Bring your radio into class one day and leave it tuned between two stations. Then sit there listening and looking extremely interested.

3. When sneezing, yell, "Ah-ah-ah-ALIEN!" Then wipe your nose and politely say, "Excuse me."

4. In front of your teacher, walk up to a friend and say, "They've detected toxic waste under the new mall, and it sure is delicious!"

5. Get a copy of Kermit the Frog singing "It's Not Easy Being Green" and play it in class.

6. Keep your desk stocked with piccolos. (Aliens hate music. Check out the book *My Teacher Is an Alien* —you'll see what I mean.)

7. Always, always, always make sure your shoes are tied in case your teacher gets mad. You might not be able to fight an alien, but you can outrun him (or her) if you zig-zag.

8. Pull off your teacher's mask during a video about reptiles!

9. Start a debate in class over the existence of alien life-forms. When it's your turn to speak, look your teacher in the eye and say "Well, I've never seen any form of intelligent life from another planet." What can he or she do?

# S-cape

Thank goodness . . . it's the end of the day at last. You have never wanted to leave school quite as badly as you do today.

*You have to get out of here. But to do so you must pass all the dots in the maze. Only then can you "S-cape" the building.*

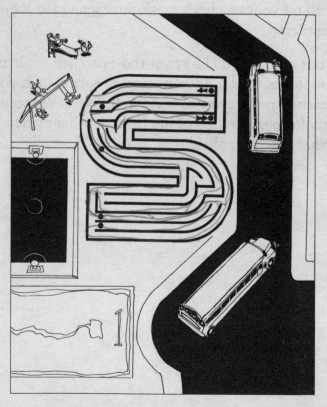

SOLUTION ON PAGE 114

# Very Punny

Tuesday night you dream you are stuck in an alien torture chamber. The aliens tell you one bad joke after another until you think you're going to crack. You wake up in a cold sweat, yelling your head off. Now you can't get these horrible jokes out of your head.

Q: What do you do with a green alien?
A: Wait until it ripens.

Q: How do you greet a two-headed alien?
A: Hello! Hello!

First Alien: That girl over there rolled her eyes at me. What should I do?
Second Alien: If you were a real gentleman, you'd pick them up and roll them right back to her!

Girl: I'm really tan from the sun!
Alien: How do you do, Really Tan. I'm Glorb from Galaxy Fourteen!

Q: Where do aliens leave their spaceships when shopping?
A: At a parking meteor!

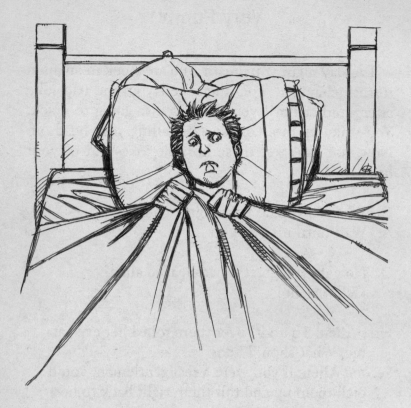

Q: How do you get an alien baby to sleep?
A: You rocket. (Rock it!)

Q: What's an alien's normal eyesight?
A: 20-20-20-20-20-20-20

Q: In what section of the newspaper are dead aliens listed?
A: In the orbit-uaries.

Q: What did the alien say to the gas pump?
A: Hey, take your finger out of your ear and listen to me!

Q: How does an extraterrestrial count to nineteen?
A: On one of its hands!

Q: Why couldn't the aliens land on the Moon?
A: Because it was full!

Planet: How are your craters?
Moon: Oh, they're depressed!

Q: What does an alien do when it gets dirty?
A: It takes a meteor shower.

Girl: Can you telephone from a spaceship?
Boy: Sure, I can tell a phone from a spaceship!

Knock, knock.
Who's there?
Athena.
Athena who?
Athena flying thaucer go by!

Q: What does an alien shave with?
A: A laser blade!

# WEDNESDAY

# Preliminary Quiz to Find Out
# If Your Classmate Is an Android

Sure, some of your friends are pretty weird. But there's a world of difference between "weird" and "remote controlled."

*Take this quiz to figure out who needs further investigation—and who's just normally strange. You know you're in trouble when:*

1. The school's most obnoxious bully
   a. makes you do his homework and then pay him for the privilege.
   b. knocks you over but then drags you to the nurse's office himself.
   c. pays for your lunch, brings the tray to your table, and feeds you every bite while humming your favorite tune.

2. The girl who thinks she's a great dresser
   a. wears a new pair of sneakers every day.
   b. stops matching her socks to her backpack.
   c. wears harem pants and a newspaper hat all week.

3. The little guy who usually tends the tadpoles in the science lab during recess

a. volunteers to write a twenty-page paper to avoid going to gym class.

b. actually shows up to play dodgeball (though he's always the first one hit anyway).

c. decides he'll make up his own one-person kickball team—and then wins the game.

4. Today in math, the class clown

a. puts pencils in his nostrils and sings "I Am the Walrus."

b. takes the pencils out of his nose.

c. uses the pencil to write out the multiplication tables up to 150.

5. At lunch, you watch out of the corner of your eye as your friend Keisha

a. eats her soup.

b. spills her soup down her shirt.

c. spoons the soup carefully into her ear.

ANSWERS ON PAGE 114

# The Principal Problem

An assembly is called. You know you've got to do SOMETHING when the principal delivers the following announcement:

*Decide whether you or a friend will fill in the blanks. Then have fun reading the final result!*

Attention, please. Can I please have your _____.
                                                                          noun

I recently overheard some _____ students
                                           adjective

_____ing in the _____, and I want to dispel any
   verb                noun

_____ that may have been _____ing. Now,
 plural noun                          verb

your teachers _____ very hard and I want you to
                     verb

treat them all like _____. All of you know that
                       plural noun

some _____ are more _____ than others.
       plural noun              adjective

You know how proud I am of my _____. I
                                              plural noun

always say you are some of the most _____ in the
                                               adjective

district. Please, try _____ not to jump to
                          adverb

_____. Thank you for your _____ and
 plural noun                          noun

_____ and please be _____ while walking back
   noun                     adjective

to your _____.
           plural noun

46

# Lab Grab

Going back to class you ponder deeply what the principal has just said. You can't quite figure it out. Then you pass the science room and are sucked in by an unknown force! Wake up! You've got to battle your way out with your wits!

*Excluding the number ten, place numbers one through nineteen in the eighteen bulbs of this puzzle. Each pair of bulbs connected by a tube must total twenty; and the three bulbs in each of the six outer sections must total thirty.*

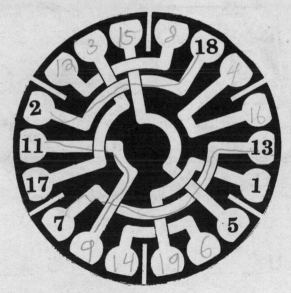

SOLUTION ON PAGE 114

# Creature Feature

Wow—that was not pleasant! You go to sit in one of the big chairs in the library to recover. Some teachers are watching a movie in there. It's kind of like something you've seen before, but not quite. Here's a scene—can you figure out the title?

T h e   U m p i r e   s t r i k e s   s h a c k

ANSWER ON PAGE 114

# The Lunchroom Incident

It's almost lunchtime and you're very hungry. Mrs. Kelso closes the copy of *The Witch of Blackbird Pond* you've all been discussing. "Okay folks," she says. "Time to go to lunch. Please don't yell in the hallways."

"I'm beyond starved," says your friend Beth. "Hey, where's Nick? He wasn't in class."

Usually, you, Beth, and Nick walk to the lunchroom together. Unlike lots of your friends, the three of you bring your lunches, though sometimes you wish you didn't. Last Friday's popcorn and butter soup had looked really interesting.

"Maybe Nick will be at his locker," you say.

"Or maybe he's been abducted," says Beth.

"Ha, ha," you say. "That's not funny."

"I know. I'm sorry," she says, as you leave the room. "Let's not even think about it."

Nick isn't at his locker either.

"Let's just go," you say to Beth. "He'll find us in the lunchroom."

The two of you sit down at your usual table. Minutes later, Henry and Eva, who buy their lunch, come over and join you.

"Can I have a piece of your cupcake?" Eva asks Beth, after Beth has set everything out neatly on the table.

"Finish your meal first and then you can have dessert," Beth teases. "Hey, look where Nick is!"

You peer over Henry's head to see Nick standing in the lunch line, looking very patient.

"Nick!" you yell. "Over here!"

Nick sees you, nods, and then turns back to the lunch display. Finally he pays and starts making his way around the other tables toward you guys.

"Wow," says Henry. "Nick never buys his lunch."

"I guess he's changed," you say, full of admiration.

Then something terrible happens. It's as if you watch it all in slow motion. A strap of a backpack is lying in the aisle. Nick steps right inside its curve and doesn't notice. He keeps walking, though his foot can't move, and—*whoa*—he lurches forward and the tray flies right out of his hands. It lands on the floor and skids a few feet, sending food everywhere. At the same time, Nick takes a trip though the air and lands in a heap, on his face, elbows, and knees.

He ends up right beneath you and Beth. And that's why the two of you are the only ones who see his chin hit the ground, causing something clear and slimy to ooze out of it. *And it's not blood.*

Everyone else is roaring with laughter, making it clear that no one else has seen what you saw.

"We have to trap him somewhere," whispers

Beth. "Before he turns the rest of us into androids, too."

"The school kitchen," you say. "Nobody's in there while food is being served."

Beth agrees with wide eyes. The two of you haul "Nick" up off the floor.

"Come on you big klutz," Beth says, "Let's get you to the nurse's office."

"Yow," he says, "That felt strange."

Nick seems kind of out of it. There's no evidence of anything weird or slimy on his chin. Everyone pretty much goes back to eating.

"You guys, I'm okay," the android says, looking at you both.

"Uh, let's just get you checked out," says Beth, putting on an I'm-your-mom-now look.

"Okay," he relents. Is his android brain telling him to play it cool? Is he receiving orders from the control center?

You lead him out of the lunchroom.

"Uh, let's stop in the kitchen and get some ice first," you say. You drag him through the big swinging doors of the kitchen.

At the same time, you and Beth realize what must be done: put him in the room where the freezer and the extra ovens are. It's a small room that locks. As far as you know there's no escape route, except for a vent in the ceiling which seems impossible to reach. Luckily, the door is open.

You figure it's because there's a big PTA party tonight at the school and they'll need blocks of ice to keep the food cool.

"But there's nobody here," protests the android. You shudder when you hear him talk, because the robot is so convincing. He sure sounds a lot like your friend Nick.

"Well—let's just step inside—" says Beth, opening the door to the little room a bit wider. Everything's happening very quickly.

"Now!" you yell. Frantically, you both push the android into the room.

"Hey!!!" he bellows, and you feel a truly unkidlike strength thrusting against the door. But you and Beth aren't weaklings. You manage to shut the door against the android, bolt it, and race out of the kitchen.

Together you go sit in the little kids' half of the playground so no one will bother you. Now that you've captured the android you don't know what to do with him (it?). You're discussing the possibilities when suddenly a shadow looms over you. It's Mr. Frank, the gym teacher.

"I understand that you played a very cruel joke on Nick Poppy," he says.

"What?" you both say. How does he know, you wonder?

"Did you or did you not lock him in the freezer?" Mr. Frank demands.

"Yes, but he—" you and Beth say at exactly the same time.

Your teacher just looks at you both. He demands you follow him to the kitchen.

You reach the kitchen. The gym teacher opens the door to the little room where the freezer is, and your stomach sinks.

There's no one inside.

One of the ovens is on, with its door open wide, sending out hot air. A small puddle of water on the floor is rapidly evaporating. You look up at the ceiling vent and see it's hanging on its hinges.

"What on earth were you doing in here, any-way?" shouts Mr. Frank. "And where's Nick?"

"But Mr. Frank," you blurt out, "Nick was an android. We locked him in here to protect the other students. But he escaped through the vent!"

Mr. Frank looks at you for a long time.

"Why don't you go sit in the principal's office," he says with a grim smile. "And stay there. Stay there until you can tell me just how the—uh—android made his escape."

How did Nick get access to the vent! Why was the oven on and what was that puddle doing in the middle of the floor! Hint: Think about what was in the room for the PTA party.

ANSWER ON PAGE 115

# Where are these people FROM?

**ACROSS**

1. Halley's _____
5. Tiny star that's much denser than the sun
6. Bright explosion of a large star, often brighter than the sun
11. Galaxy or candy bar
12. Space organization based in Florida
13. *Third* _____ *From the Sun*
14. The brightest and most distant objects in the universe
15. Color of Mars
16. Number of planets in our solar system
17. Movie with two sequels: *Star* _____

**DOWN**

1. Bowl-shaped hole in the ground
2. Movie alien who phones home
3. Astronauts travel in a space_____
4. Word that means star system
7. Seventh planet from the sun
8. Type of rocket fuel
9. This is created when a massive star burns out
10. Planet with majestic rings
11. _____ in the moon
13. Location-finding device

SOLUTION ON PAGE 115

55

# Alien Trivia Quiz

Think you're a big expert on aliens now? Maybe you have learned something during the last few days of school—even if it's not the three R's. Evaluate yourself with this quiz.

1. An alien's favorite hobby is
   a. working on his saucer.
   b. playing "Trivial Earthling Pursuit."
   c. gamma-ray nostril blast target practice.

2. When an alien sneezes, it's best to
   a. offer him a tissue.
   b. dive into a hole in the ground and stay there.
   c. say "Gesundheit!" (He'll understand— he has a universal translator!)

3. What well-known person will an alien point to and say "He's definitely one of us"?
   a. Darth Vader
   b. Michael Jackson
   c. E.T.

4. Ancient history question: A long time ago, rock star David Bowie became famous by pretending he was from outer space. Actually, we're not sure he was pretending. What did he call himself?

a. Sigfried Roy
b. Sigmund Freud
c. Ziggy Stardust

5. What was the alien teacher's real name in Bruce Coville's book *My Teacher Is an Alien?*
a. Bolshcvik
b. Broxholm
c. Branflakes

6. Who was the fattest alien in the Star Wars trilogy?
a. Barney the Dinosaur
b. Jabba the Hut
c. John the Goodman

7. Residents of which planet tend to get teased the most at interplanetary conventions?
a. Mercury
b. Earth
c. Uranus

8. Before the days of Captain Jean-Luc Picard, the characters of Star Trek were led by a man with hair. His namc was:
a. Captain Jerk
b. Captain Kirk
c. Captain Crunch

ANSWERS ON PAGE 115

# Right Down the Middle

Your friend Nathan has always been obsessed with movies and TV shows with aliens in them. After lunch, you find some strange blank lines carved into his desk and know it must be important.

1. Peter, Susan, and Duncan's original alien teacher (You should know this one by now!)
2. The planet that the title *Third Rock from the Sun* refers to
3. Author of *My Teacher Is an Alien* series (last name)
4. Actress in trio of *Alien* movies (first name)
5. Kryptonite was the one thing that could hurt him
6. Klingons and _____
7. Mulder and Scully investigate the unexplained on *The* _____
8. Robocop was one of these
9. *Star Trek*'s logician
10. In what movie did aliens invade on a holiday?
11. This alien really wanted to keep in touch.

ANSWERS ON PAGE 115

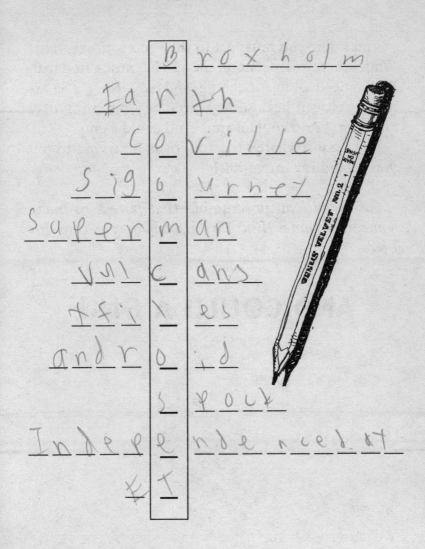

Broxholm

Earth

Coville

Sigourney

Superman

Vulcans

Titles

android

spout

Independenny

ET

# Brain Drain

You know you must get to the broom closet—fast! Wait—there's someone in there! He's stuck in a really strange-looking machine and you can't see his head. You can hear some words he's repeating over and over: "And could a gnu? And could a gnu?"

Has he just visited the zoo, or is he trying to tell you something important?

*See if you can unscramble that phrase to make someone's name! Hint: He's already appeared in this book.*

# AND COULD A GNU

ANSWER ON PAGE 116

# Wall Eyes

In the bathroom you notice some new graffiti. Somehow, you get the feeling that it's watching you.

*What is it?*

ANSWER ON PAGE 116

# Stuck On You

Wednesday night you dream you're stuck in a giant paper clip! This has got to be the work of an alien teacher!

*See if you can get from ON to OFF.*

SOLUTION ON PAGE 116

# THURSDAY

# Shock-A-Block

You drop your little sister off at the kindergarten room. Is there something wrong with her alphabet blocks today?

ANSWER ON PAGE 116

# Compound Confusion

Your friend Ariana comes into your first period class babbling. She says she was late for HOMEPET, that Susan Simmons is a TEACHER'S TIME, and that her dog ate her LUNCHWORK! See if you can figure out the rest of what Ariana says by mixing and matching different first and second parts of the compound words below. Each first word goes with only one other second word.

*Among the words is the thing that scared Ariana out of her wits!*

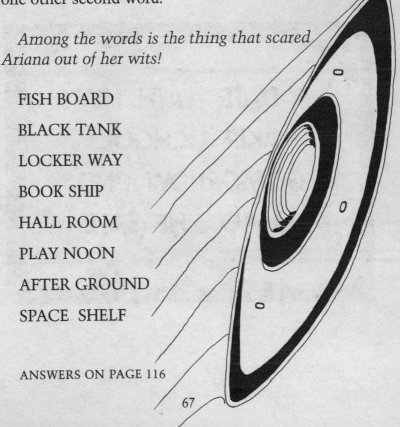

FISH BOARD

BLACK TANK

LOCKER WAY

BOOK SHIP

HALL ROOM

PLAY NOON

AFTER GROUND

SPACE SHELF

ANSWERS ON PAGE 116

# Code Crazy

Gretchen and Maia are missing from math class. You find this note under your desk. You recognize Gretchen's handwriting. She must have dropped the note yesterday. You try to figure out what it says.

*Can you decipher Gretchen and Maia's secret code? Trying to read it aloud may help.*

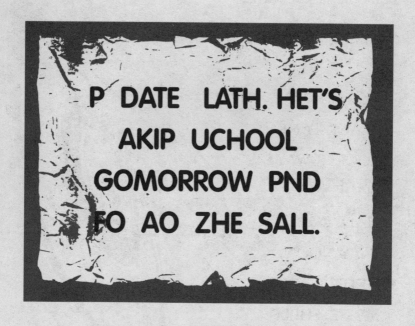

ANSWER ON PAGE 117

# Vent Event

In math you're staring at the ceiling vents, which you think might turn out to be convenient escape routes. It'll be a tight squeeze, but when you're desperate, anything goes. You just have to figure out which one is bigger.

*Can you figure out which is the bigger vent?*

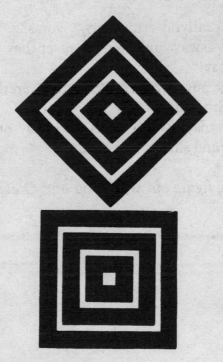

ANSWER ON PAGE 117

# Cow Latin ??!?

You try to come up with a language that the aliens' Universal Translator won't understand. A-ha! You have it! You turn to your friend Gretchen and say:

"I-ay awsay issMay osinskykay ewingchay a-ay othballmay odaytay."

"Ou'reyay iddingkay!" she says, catching on immediately.

"I'm-ay otallytay erious-say," you say. "I-ay ought-thay it-ay asway andycay utbay enthay I-ay awsay the-ay oxbay!"

"Owhay anymay lienssay are-ay erethay?" your friend Jill interrupts.

"I-ay on'tday owknay. Otslay anday otslay," says Gretchen, and shakes her head.

*Can you figure out what you and Gretchen said?*

TRANSLATION ON PAGE 117

# Net Escape

In gym, you see this design painted over the basketball net.

*Can you figure out what it means? Hint: It's something you might want to run for!*

ANSWER ON PAGE 117

# Mixed Message

An amazing thing happens. The biggest creep in school gets up at lunch and says:

"Um, hey, everybody. I know you all think I'm a

_____ . But now that there are _____ aliens
  noun                                     adjective

everywhere I have something _____ to say. I'm
                                         adjective

really sorry if I've _____ your _____ , or
                      verb—past tense       plural noun

made you _____ , or _____ your _____ .
         adjective       verb—past tense      plural noun

Cuz I now know I'm just as _____ as you are.
                              adjective

Maybe if we all _____ _____ , we can _____
                 verb      adverb           verb

the aliens together. I swear if you guys let me join

you in this one I'll never _____ your _____
                       verb       plural noun

again!

*Find a friend and—you know the rest.*

# The Telephone Cipher

You realize that the creep is right (even though you could barely understand him). There is strength in numbers. The whole school should have a code that everybody can learn and use quickly, when needed. Susan comes up with the telephone code, since everyone has a telephone.

*On every telephone there are both numbers and letters. Each of the numbers on the telephone goes with three letters: 2= A, B, C; 7= P, R, S, and so on. So, the telephone code will be made up of different combinations of the numbers 2, 3, 4, 5 ,6 , 7, 8, and 9. Each number will represent one of three different letters.*

*(Nobody said it was THAT easy!)*

*Here are some samples you can train the troops on:*

Get help! (438  4357)
Alien in the library! (25436  46  843  5427279)
Gross! (47677)

*Here are some to try:*
3668  46  86  278  25277!
3825!
33247437 8447 3278!

ANSWERS ON PAGE 117

# How Not To Be a Ding-a-ling

Speaking of telephones, you heard a rumor that the aliens want to kidnap the most typical, normal, average kids in the class. This is pretty much what you are, so your options are: act really, really dumb, or act really, really smart. You're too embarrassed to act really, really dumb, (and besides if this is all a hoax you'd end up with bad grades for no reason) so you ask your friend who loves tricks and games how you can prove you've got an incredible memory. He tells you about the telephone book trick and you can't wait to show it to your teacher! Practice a little with a friend first.

*Get a phone book, a pencil, and a piece of paper. Give your friend the pencil and paper. Then tell him or her to do the following:*

1. *Think of any three-digit number—with each digit different than the other two—and write it down without showing you. She shouldn't tell you the number. Each of the three digits should be different.*
2. *Reverse the digits.*
3. *Subtract the smaller number from the larger one. (For instance, if the number is 349, the reversed number is 943. So 943 minus 349 equals 594.)*
4. *Reverse the digits of the new number. (In our example, reversing the digits in 594 gives you 495.)*
5. *Add up the two three-digit numbers, from 2. and 3. ( 594 plus 495, to get 1089.)*

The key to this trick is the number 1089. The instructions you gave your friend are based on a mathematical formula. If everything's done correctly, the result will always equal the number 1089. That is your secret.

6. *Take the last two digits in the answer. Turn to that page in the telephone book.*
7. *Take the first two digits in the number and count down that number of lines from the top of the first column on the page. When your friend's finger has stopped on a particular name, amaze her by telling her what name it is.*

How is this done? Since the final result of the math will always be 1089, you can find out beforehand which name is the 10th name in the first column on page 89. These are the directions you just gave your friend. Just remember that name, and when the time comes, you will be ready with the correct answer.

Since the name will always be the same no matter how many times you do the trick, you obviously cannot perform this trick more than once to the same person.

# Oldy But Goody

In Science the teacher slips a tape into the VCR. When an image comes onto the screen she looks very embarrassed and immediately ejects the tape. Not too many kids noticed what the scene was—but you did. And you know the title of the movie.

*Can you figure it out?*

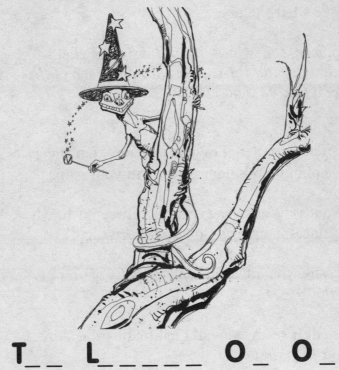

T _ _ L _ _ _ _ _ O _ O _

ANSWER ON PAGE 117

# Slippery Sayings

Your home ec teacher seems really nice, but you've noticed that she talks a little strangely. For instance, yesterday she said, "Girls are made of pancakes and lice and everything nice" and she didn't seem to be joking. You've also heard other almost familiar but just-not-quite-right phrases come out of her mouth. You decide to try correcting her during class today and see what she does.

*Replace the words in italics with the word it should be. Hint: the correct fill-in for each of these is either a food or a body part.*

1. "Thank you, Jen. I'm glad to know that the *gasoline* of human kindness flows in your veins."

2. "What's the answer to number three, Josh? My goodness, you're as slow as *toothpaste*."

3. "Leslie, you are beginning to really get on my *scalp*!"

4. "Well! It seems you all qualified by the skin of your *fingernails*!"

5. "When things get discouraging, it's important to keep your *elbow* up."

6. "When the holidays come we'll learn that song about the partridge in the *grape* tree."

7. "My advice to you is not to put all your *pebbles* in one basket."

8. "Does everyone know the song about the lady with rings on her *ears* and bells on her *eyeballs*?"

9. "Oh, don't worry so much, Andrew! At your age life should be just a bowl of *walnuts*!"

10. "Does everyone know the story of the princess and the *peanut*?"

11. "Study hard, Ashley, because one day you'll be the one bringing home the *balloon*."

ANSWERS ON PAGE 118

# It Could Be Worse

On the bus going home, you realize that when you think about it, things really are pretty good here. . . .

BEING AT SCHOOL
games in gym class
squaredancing
moonwalking
peer pressure
music class
a fun class trip to the aquarium
blowing the wrappers off straws
eating lunch in the cafeteria

VS

VS.

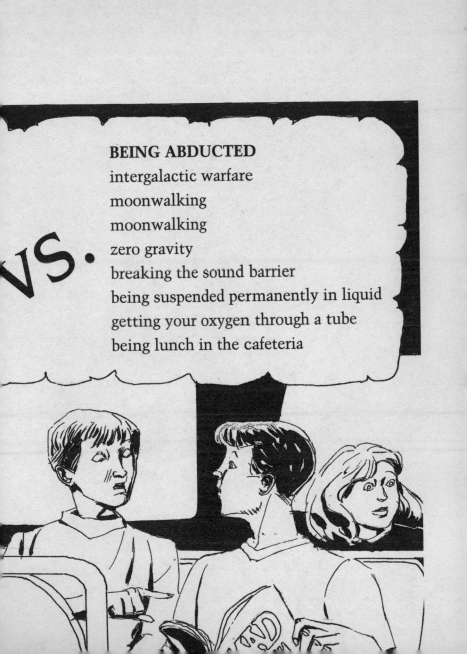

# FRIDAY

# Locker Shocker

You come into school a little late. You open your locker and . . .

# Slime Rhyme

You quickly go to your first period art class. You open the door, expecting everybody to stare at you—but the classroom is completely empty! Crumpled on Ms. Richards' desk is what seems to be a love poem from one alien to another.

*Find anyone you can to fill in the blanks—FAST!*

How the _____ _____ shines on your _____
            adjective      noun               noun

of green.

You're the slimiest _____ _____ I've ever
                      adjective      noun

seen.

I can't wait to see you _____ under the _____
                    verb             number

moons, or hear the _____ _____ as the
                 noun      verb

_____ croons.
 noun

I'd kidnap _____ of these _____ earth crea-
         number            adjective

tures for you, with your spiky _____
                             adjective

_____ and your _____ of blue.
 plural noun          noun

# Pix Tricks #2

You look up from the love note, confused and feeling sicker than ever. Something's written in pictures on the blackboard.

*Can you decipher your art teacher's message?*

ANSWER ON PAGE 118

# Terror in the Teachers' Lounge
## A MINI MYSTERY

Oh, no. This must mean that your art teacher is an alien. You think with a twinge of embarassment of all the pictures of spaceships and space creatures she must have secretly laughed at throughout her career! You also realize, though, that that note for you on the board means she must have felt something for her pathetic earthly pupils.

You decide one thing: you don't want to "escape while you can." You've got to find the spaceship. That's where your art teacher is, and that's where your classmates are.

You leave the art room. The hall feels very empty. You pass by Susan Simmons' locker, which is wide open. This really worries you. Nobody leaves their locker door open like that. Could Susan herself have been abducted, even with her expert knowledge of aliens and proven skill at the piccolo?

Your stomach starts to hurt. You wonder for a second if you're scared enough for your knees to knock together. It happens in books that way.

You pass the library and there's no librarian at the desk—a sight you have never seen in your many years at this school. Your heart starts to pound. Where is everybody? Are you, by some fluke, the only one left? "And how does this make you feel?" you imagine the school nurse asking.

"Well," you imagine answering, "pretty awful!!"

Then, across from the teachers' lounge, you stop. Did you just hear something? You walk towards the door—very, very slowly. Will this be a clue? Or are these slow steps going to be your last? Should you yank open the door and see what's going on in there? Or should you just run?

You close your eyes for a second. Then you open the door. Inside, across the room, four people turn to face you: Howard, a kid from math class who is always looking at your paper; Mr. Frank, the gym teacher; Tom, a kid from your reading class—and Ms. Richards, the art teacher.

Before you can say anything, Ms. Richards shouts, "Go away, it's . . . it's dangerous here!" and shakes her head at you violently.

You look at her and then look away. You're determined to stay.

"You're going to . . . escape, aren't you?" you say to Tom and Howard. By now you're quaking.

"Escape? Escape from what?" asks Mr. Frank, glancing at Ms. Richards. "We've just been relaxing. I was just about to bring these boys down to the gym for some b-ball practice."

You look at him. You're a little insulted that he thinks you'll believe him. You take another step inside. The room which usually looks so comfortable now seems full of awful secrets. The water cooler blubs ominously.

"Tell me where the entrance to the spaceship is," you say. "NOW!"

The gym teacher roars with laughter. You flinch as he starts moving towards you.

"You sad little creature!" he says. "No earthling comes onto the ship without our permission!"

Obviously he doesn't care any longer if you know he's an alien.

"Listen," interrupts Ms. Richards. "There's a portal to the ship in the library and there's one in the broom closet. But you won't be able to operate either of them! Now go away! Run home, little earthling!"

"Kavillian!" yells the alien who was your gym teacher. He yells it at the alien who was your art teacher. "How could you tell . . . are you crazy?"

"Mirgibbi, please!" Kavillian (Ms. Richards) shouts back. "Please work with me on this one! You aren't the only being with two brains around here!"

"Fine." Mirgibbi (Mr. Frank) looks at you. "It doesn't matter. So we'll have an extra earthling. It can't hurt. Go try the portal in the library, kid. It's easier than the one in the broom closet."

Then Tommy, the kid from reading class, who's been totally silent this whole time, clears his throat. He's looking a little strange. "The portal is in only one place," he says, and coughs.

"THESE ANDROIDS!" screams Mirgibbi, looking at Tommy. He smacks his forehead and makes his face wobble in a way that makes you queasy. "You just CAN'T program them to lie! I just refuse to believe there isn't software for lying these days!"

"Be quiet, Mirgibbi!" snaps Kavillian.

Her anxiety gives you the tiniest bit of hope. If they can be coaxed to say enough, maybe you can piece their hints together and find out where the portal really is. You walk further towards the little group.

"Howard, help me out here," you say, looking hard at him. You know that Howard has never said a true word in his life. He looks at you, terrified. He must have been kidnapped—he's too scared to be an android.

"What Mr. Frank and Tommy said is true," Howard says.

"Oh, my," sighs your former art teacher, putting her head in her hands.

Does her "oh, my" mean that now you have enough information to find the entrance to the spaceship? It just might.

*You know the portal is either in the library or the broom closet. If Howard always lies, and if androids can only tell the truth, can you figure out which place to investigate further?*

ANSWER ON PAGE 118

# Star Wars

You open the door to the broom closet, go inside—you're instantaneously transported through space. As if by magic, you find yourself at the entrance to the spaceship. As you make your way across the ship's outer shell, a flaming number-comet comes flying at you! If you can figure it out before it hits, the comet will turn to ash. But if you can't do it fast enough, you and your rescue mission will be zapped into oblivion!

*There are thirty-seven stars in this comet. Beginning with star number one, consecutively number every star so that you end at star #37. You may only go from one adjacent star tip to the next, and you can't revisit any star.*

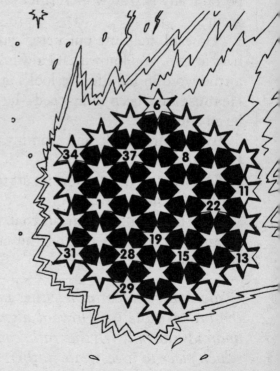

**ANSWER ON PAGE 118**

# Up Close and Personal

At last you're inside. Now what?

Exploring as quietly as you can, you come upon what seems to be a giant TV. It looks like a reporter has gotten aboard and is conducting an interview!

Reporter: All these dials and controls . . . are these for steering the ship?

Alien: No, this is a giant flying microwave and this stuff is to make sure that dinner turns out okay. Duh!

R: So, why are you visiting Earth?

A: I'm visiting your little blue ball of mud to get some prime specimens.

R: Specimens of what?

A: I mean . . . uh . . . spacemen! We want to learn from your astronauts—not!

R: You can't fool me. I heard you say "specimens."

A: Did not.

R: Did too.

A: Did not.

R: Okay fine. I'll change the subject. Why do you listen to that horrible screechy music?

A: You listen to Alanis Morissette, do you not?

R: Point taken. Now, tell me: do the young on your planet go to school?

A: We implant what you would call a computer chip into heads at an early age. I can't believe the way you guys do it on Earth—thirteen years or more down the drain! And all that chalk dust! When I was filling in for a teacher, chalk got caught between my mask and my face . . .

R: Uh-huh. Since you've had firsthand experience (clears throat), what are your impressions of how we educate our kids on Earth?

A: Most of the time, your kids should be educating you. They don't start wars. They don't drive huge land vehicles that pollute your atmosphere. They don't wear high heels out of choice. Or neckties.

R: Well! For your information we often have to wear this stuff to work! Sheesh. Let me ask one more thing. What are your thoughts on our computers, our CD-ROM games, the Internet . . .?

A: (laughter)

R: What's so funny?

A: (more laughter)

R: WHAT??

A: (sobbing with laughter) You guys are clueless! Stick to those cute portable paper things. You know: books! (more laughter) You ask THE DUMBEST QUESTIONS!

R: I've had enough of this. Enough. Thanks a lot. When are you going to let me off this spaceship thing, anyway?

A: That's the dumbest question you've asked yet!

# Blue in the Face

Telling yourself you can watch as much TV as you want when you get home, you continue your search. You enter a room where Susan, Duncan, Peter, a girl who's sat next to you in English for years, a guy who always beats you at basketball, his little brother, and lots of other kids are held frozen in blue forcefields! A strange puzzle is etched onto their pedestals. Above the puzzle, written in many languages, most of which are not earthly, is: *Your journey through this lock must produce 100 points.* You shudder, then look around you. You advance towards your classmates very slowly.

"Simply stand on your head while you think about it," says a blue alien with a white humanlike moustache who has suddenly materialized.

*To get 100 points you must go through the maze, passing numbers that add up to 100 without recrossing your tracks. With a hint like the blue alien's, you're sure to succeed.*

ANSWER ON PAGE 119

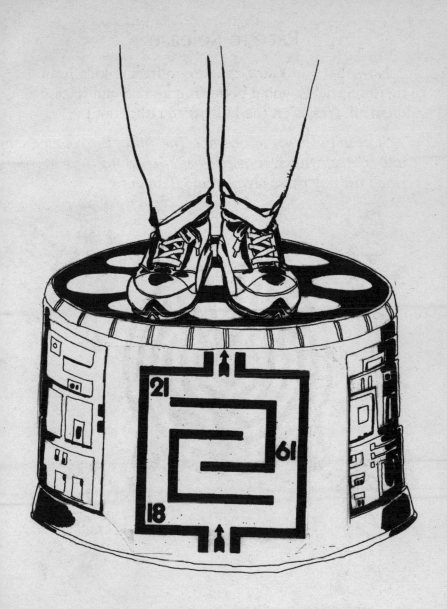

# Race to Release

Now that you know the key to freeing kids from their forcefields, you'd better run around and release them all. (Yes, even the kids you'd rather not.)

*Start in the lower left corner. The object is to come into contact with every circle before reaching the end. Don't use any passageway more than once.*

**ANSWER ON PAGE 119**

# Required Reading

A troop of alien guards come down the hallway. You and the other kids crowd into a room. Could this possibly be a library? Check out some of the titles:

TRYING TO LAND SAFELY
Major Catastrophe

A TRIP TO GALAXY 14
Miles A. Way

HOW TO BECOME A SPACE EXPLORER
I.C. Stars

LET'S FLY AT THE SPEED OF LIGHT
Hugo First

PARACHUTING FROM SPACESHIPS
Willie Makit

TAKING OFF
Europe N. Daway

MY LIFE IN THE OUTER REACHES OF THE GALAXY
I. Malone

GODOP Eoop AHHIOrp
Marsh Inn

# Groovy Movie

Boy, are those aliens calm! As you dash by a room you see a bunch watching a movie. It sounds like something you've seen before—but weirder.

*Can you figure it out?*

C _ _ _   A _ _ _ _ _

ANSWER ON PAGE 119

On another one of those large-screen TV's, you see a gap-toothed alien sitting behind a desk, holding up a top-ten list.

## Top Ten Reasons
## We Should Let Humans Live

1. Dennis Rodman may be one of us.
2. Earthling beauty parlors are great for genuine facial peels!
3. Who else could make such lame movies about us?
4. Betting on how long they'll last on a spaceship before they implode is a good way to pass the time.
5. Being called "superior beings" is a real ego boost.
6. The look on their faces when you say, "Take me to your leader!"
7. When you play hockey with them and it's time for a "face-off"—well, you get the idea.
8. There's no such thing as a non-earthling who can make decent waffles.
9. The masks we model after their hideous faces really scare the neighbors back home!
10. People are aliens too.

# Knowledge is Power

All the kids you've released are crowding around you. This is not good. They should all get off the spaceship as fast as possible. It would be awful if they got recaptured. Some of the littler kids are crying.

"Go! Run!" you say, feeling desperate.

"Why aren't you going anywhere?" says a tall boy.

You take a deep breath. "I have a mission I want to complete," you say. "I want to make sure the aliens don't take any information about Earth back to their home planet. I'm going to find the information they've gathered and then steal it—or erase it!"

Everyone stares at you.

"The laser-plank, which you need to get off the ship, is in the hold," you say. "You're almost there!"

"Where?" asks a girl whose name you don't know.

You carefully explain how to get down to the exit laser-plank, rather amazed at yourself for knowing. You have been running around the spaceship for a while now and parts of it are becoming familiar. Then you find Peter and ask him to lead the way. When everyone finally trails off after him, you sigh with relief.

Now you wonder where the aliens have stored the information. It really could be anywhere. Maybe you could find Ms. Richards, your old art teacher, and ask her. Of course, she's an alien, but she has a soft spot for humans. You start off in search of her. Suddenly the blue alien with the white moustache (the one who gave you a hint about the release of the prisoners) materializes in front of you.

"You want to erase the information we have about you earthlings from our knowledge bank, I think," he says.

You nod your head, feeling small. How does he know? you wonder. Did he overhear you speaking? Or overhear you thinking?

"However," the blue alien continues, looking at you with bulgy eyes, "I am the one who values this information more than anyone. I am the one who compiled it."

You gulp. Maybe this was the wrong guy to run into at this particular moment, with your particular goal.

"However again," he says, curling his moustache (you are struck by how Earthlike some of his gestures are),"I feel that some congratulations are in order. You and your friends have been unexpectedly successful at discovering the truth about us. You have unravelled tricks and solved puzzlcs that should have kept you comfortably in the dark. The fact that you are here at all impresses me very much."

You stand there. Where are these compliments leading?

"I will show you where the information is," he says. "But you will have to figure out how to transport it."

Your heart races with excitement and you begin to thank him.

He silences you with a pudgy hand in the air. "Come," he says.

Together you descend to the information hold at the bottom of the spaceship. It is cold and very dark, with small bright lights everywhere. The blue alien leads you to the right, then stops and presses one of the small lights on the floor with his foot. Three black spheres rise out of cavities in the floor and start to roll towards you.

"These are the Earth information pods," says the alien, stopping them with his foot. "If you put three of your fingers into these three holes—don't be scared, now—you will see some of the images collected inside. Go ahead."

You aren't quite sure whether to laugh or cry at how much these things resemble bowling balls. You put your fingers inside the holes in one of the pods and suddenly find yourself watching a class in session: Mr. Suransky's Social Studies class. He's talking about the American Revolution. "Sarah, I want you to be Benedict Arnold," he's saying in his slow, deliberate voice. "Now, you're about to betray your country. . . ."

You take your fingers out of the holes. Seeing the class makes you sad. Will you ever see any of those people again?

Then you feel a trembling below your feet and your heart sinks. The spaceship is preparing to take off.

As if reading your mind (is he reading your mind?) the blue alien says, "The ship is preparing to leave your planet. The laser-plank to the ground is still usable, though."

Without taking your eyes off him, you gather up the three pods and hold them awkwardly in your arms.

"Yes," says the alien, "hurry over to the laser-plank. It is getting weaker and weaker as we prepare for take off. It can only support"—he does a few calculations on a small square object that makes bleeping noises—"seventy-five pounds. Now, I'm not sure what you weigh, but each info-pod weighs fifteen pounds. You will definitely not be able to carry all of them, and possibly none of them."

You want to cry.

"There is a way, little one," says the alien.

Suddenly a round hole opens in the side of the room. It's a portal, and you can actually see grass far, far beneath you. The laser-plank glows all the way down to the ground but you can see it's getting thinner and thinner.

"There is a way to escape without leaving any information behind," says the blue alien. He disappears.

How can you get down the laser-plank with all three info-pods, when the plank will hold only seventy-five pounds?

ANSWER ON PAGE 119

# Epilogue

You're home. Your parents have gone out to a movie and left you to babysit your little sister. The two of you go to the corner to pick up a pizza. You walk with your little sister's hand in yours, thinking about all that's happened to you and your friends in the last week.

Walking home through the deepening twilight you keep your gaze in front of you. You don't feel like looking at the stars right now.

At home the light's blinking on the answering machine. You reach out to press it and then you stop. The light's never blinked that way before . . . it's going on and off in a complicated pattern. Your heart sinks.

You press the button with a trembling finger to hear what's on the tape.

"Greetings, children," sounds a metallic voice. You gulp.

"By the time you hear this we will be far, far away. It is true that you now have all the information we gathered about Earthlings. But one of us managed to memorize this phone number. We just wanted to say that we have truly been impressed by the hidden abilities of human children. We will therefore now beam you a very important uncoded chunk of information called the . . ."

*Go ahead—turn the page!*

# Answer Key

**page 2**

Answers to the Preliminary Quiz To Determine If Your Teacher Is an Alien

Mostly a's: That's the way it goes, kids.

Mostly b's: A pretty good day, wouldn't you say?

Mostly c's: We wouldn't ordinarily say this, but CLOSE THE BOOK NOW. RUN!

**page 5**

The teacher on the bottom left.

**page 6**

SEARCH THE CLASSROOM DURING RECESS FOR THE X-RAY GLASSES.

**page 7**

MEET ME AT MY LOCKER. I HAVE SOMETHING TO TELL YOU ABOUT MRS. HOWARD.

Code Breaker: Start reading in the lower right-hand corner.

**page 11**

There has to be a fourth of July in France. The French don't just skip from the third of July to the fifth, do they? Hmm. Why doesn't Ms. Love know this?

**page 12**

The noodles, an optical illusion, are "flipping" to face first one way and then the other.

**page 13**

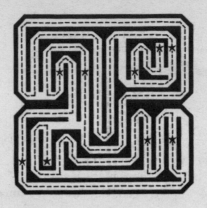

**page 15**
*She will kidnap five pupils.*

**page 18**
The alien teacher is trying to remember these facts about life on Earth. There are:

13 Stripes on the American Flag — 50 States in the United States
9 Planets in the Solar System — 12 Months in a Year
7 Days in a Week — 3 Strikes and You're Out!
4 Fingers and 1 Thumb

**page 19**
The following sixty-four words can be made out of the word "nothingness." (That's not even including plurals.) There may be more. Who knows?

| | | | |
|---|---|---|---|
| eight | goes | hiss | inset |
| ghost | gone | hog | into |
| gin | gosh | hoist | is |
| gist | hinge | hose | isn't |
| gneiss | hint | host | it |
| go | his | in | nest |

| net | nosh | shin | singe | then |
| night | not | shine | site | thin |
| nine | note | shoe | snot | thing |
| ninth | nothing | shot | son | this |
| nit | on | sight | sonnet | thong |
| no | one | sign | sting | those |
| noise | onset | sine | stone | tinge |
| none | sent | sing | tennis | tone |

**page 20**

These steps could not really exist. They make up an optical illusion.

**page 25**

The headlights make up another "flip-flop" optical illusion!

**page 26**

In the teacher's lounge are a bunch of TEENAGE MUTANT NINJA TEACHERS.

**page 27**

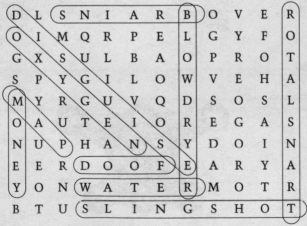

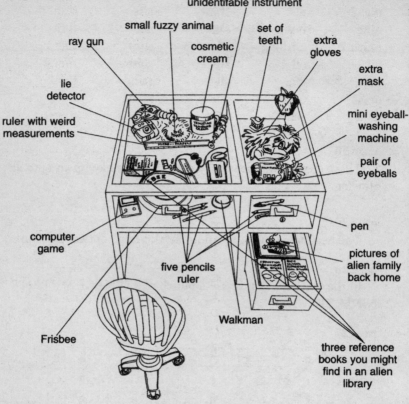

unidentifiable instrument

small fuzzy animal

set of teeth

ray gun

cosmetic cream

extra gloves

extra mask

lie detector

ruler with weird measurements

mini eyeball-washing machine

pair of eyeballs

computer game

pen

five pencils ruler

pictures of alien family back home

Frisbee

Walkman

three reference books you might find in an alien library

**page 30**

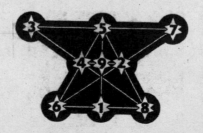

Peter knows that Mr. Forsythe has never been to Argentina because the sub was talking about it being cold there in the wintertime. In the Southern Hemisphere, where Argentina is located, seasons are the opposite to ours. Summer is cold, and winter—you guessed it—is hot.

**page 35**

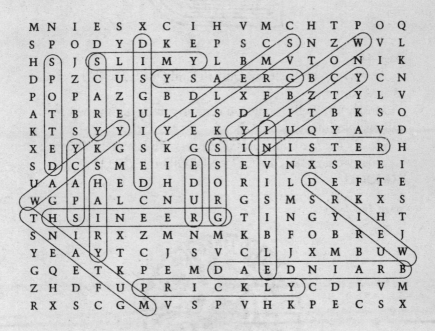

**page 38**

**page 44**

Answers to Preliminary Quiz to Find Out If Your Classmate is an Android

Mostly a's: Well! People are certainly living up to their reputations! Nothing to worry about.

Mostly b's: Medium normalcy. Everyone has their off-days.

Mostly c's: EMERGENCY! ANDROID-INFESTED SCHOOL!

**page 47**

**page 48**

The movie is called *The Umpire Strikes Shack*.

**page 53**

To reach the vent in the ceiling, "Nick" the android must have stood on the blocks of ice being stored in the room for the PTA meeting. He turned on the oven so that the ice would melt after he'd escaped, erasing the evidence. That's what the puddle on the floor was—melted ice.

**page 54**

Crossword puzzle answers:

Across: 1. COMET  5. WHITE DWARF  6. SUPERNOVA
11. MILKY WAY 12. NASA 13. ROCK
14. QUASAR 15. RED 16. NINE 17. WARS

Down: 1. CRATER 2. ET 3. SHIP  4. GALAXY  7. URANUS
8. OIL 9. BLACK HOLE 10. SATURN  11. MAN
13. RADAR

**page 56**

Alien Trivia Quiz

If you took the quiz and didn't notice that the correct answer is almost always "b", retake quiz.

**page 59**

|        |   |              |
|-------:|:-:|:-------------|
|        | B | roxholm      |
|     Ea | R | th           |
|      C | O | ville        |
|    Sig | O | urney        |
|  Super | M | an           |
|    Vul | C | ans          |
|   X Fi | L | es           |
|   andr | O | id           |
|        | S | pock         |
|  Indep | E | ndence Day   |
|      E | T |              |

115

**page 60**

"And could a gnu?" unscrambles into the name Duncan Dougal.

**page 62**

The grafitti in the bathroom actually says "EYE."

**page 63**

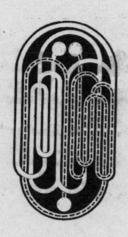

**page 66**

These blocks are optical illusions. They could not really exist as they are shown.

**page 67**

FISH TANK
BLACKBOARD
LOCKER ROOM
HALLWAY
PLAYGROUND
AFTERNOON
SPACESHIP—the word that scared Ariana out of her wits!
BOOKSHELF

**page 68**

Well, it looks like two kids have a "normal" reason for not being in school! What a relief. The note says:

I HATE MATH. LET'S SKIP SCHOOL TOMORROW AND GO TO THE MALL.

Code Breaker: They simply replaced the first letter of every word with another, randomly chosen letter.

**page 69**

The vents in the ceiling are exactly the same size.

**page 70**

Pig Latin translation:
I saw Miss Kosinsky chewing a mothball today.
You're kidding!
I'm totally serious. I thought it was candy but then I saw the box!
How many aliens are there?
I don't know. Lots and lots.

**page 71**

The design over the basketball net says "LIFE."

**page 73**

The answers to the telephone cipher are:
Don't go to art class!
Duck!
Decipher this fast!

**page 77**

The movie's title is *The Lizard of Oz*.

**page 79**

1. milk
2. molasses
3. nerves
4. teeth
5. chin
6. pear
7. eggs
8. fingers, toes
9. cherries
10. pea
11. bacon

**page 87**

*Kids leaving in spaceship. Escape while you can.*

**page 91**

Howard, the human boy who always lies, said, "What Mr. Frank and Tommy said is true." But we also know that Tommy, the android, only speaks the truth. Therefore only "Mr. Frank" was lying. What did he say? That "the portal in the library" was easier. Go to the broom closet. See what you can find!

CONGRATULATIONS! You've just found the secret code to unlock the *My Teacher Is an Alien* CD-ROM game on the web! The code is: BROOM CLOSET

**page 92**

**page 97**

If you turn the maze upside down, the numbers 18 and 61 flip over to become 81 and 19. Ignoring the upside-down 21, add 81 and 19 together to get 100!

**page 98**

**page 100**

This movie is called *Comb Alone*.

**page 106**

You can juggle the info-pods. That way, you are holding only one at once—and the other two will be in the air!

1369